Katie Morgan

Never the LOT

Illustrations by Fiona Dulieu

First hardback edition October 2019

First softback edition October 2019

Illustrations by Fiona Dulieu Copyright © Fiona Dulieu 2019

Edited by Amy McLean

Back cover photo by Dottie Photography

ISBN 978-0-578-59619-8

Library of Congress Control Number:
2019914960

Dedicated to my son,
the greatest thing I've ever done.
I love you, Lennon.

On a hill overlooking a pasture blanketed in snow

Grew a small pine seedling that was nervous to grow.

He was planted with a purpose, to grow up to be

Adorned with decorations like Christmas royalty.

Planted by a farmer who well understood

That pine trees were more than a pile of wood.

Surrounding him were others, planted the same day as he,

Formed around him in rows like perfect geometry.

"Look," said one. "Look up to the sky.

There is the future for you and for I."

Above them a great billboard showed a Christmas tree, with words

Selling trees to tree lots by the dozen in herds.

Oh! The tree on the billboard, how fantastic she looked.

A fantasy, an ambition, a direction, they were hooked.

Decorated with lights, ornaments and tinsel of red,

With a beautiful star crowned on her head.

All the other saplings planted around him in rows

Spoke only of how good they would look in their Christmas bows.

And how they dreamt of that precious day coming,

When someone would take them and amount them to something.

To be admired by children of all ages and sizes,

To protect all the presents, the candy and prizes.

But something about the picture didn't sit quite right with our friend.

Something seemed strange. Like she was being strangled with trim.

Her face seemed distorted as if she felt pain.

She appeared thirsty, as if she could no longer remain.

He shrugged it off and kept these thoughts to himself,

And continued to chatter about Santa and his elves.

The seasons changed and the weather became cold.

Enough time had passed that the saplings grew old.

They had become trees and were now old enough

To start their destiny of being decorated with fluff.

Then the day came, as it did every year,

When one tree would be chosen to start holiday cheer.

The farmer that raised them came up to their hill,

To pick the best tree for at home by the window sill.

When the farmer reached the hill, he spent time looking around

For the perfect Christmas tree that could remove any frown.

All the trees held their breath and tried not to move,

As the farmer looked at each one like art at the Louvre.

"This one has a bald spot," he said to a few.

"Ah yes, but this one is full. It shall do."

He stopped at a beautiful tree three rows from our friend,

Pulled out a saw, told the tree she'd reached the end.

But no one had heard him say such a thing,

No one, of course, but our dear old sapling.

The other trees were too jealous. "How could this be?

That the farmer chose her and did not choose me?"

But the sapling paid attention as the farmer cut her loose;

Her face looked strangled like her throat were in a noose.

Her eyes closed immediately as if in a sleep,

While the farmer dragged her trunk down that hill steep.

The tracks that she left from being dragged through the snow

Reminded our sapling of a brave march to death row.

Not much time passed until she was on her perch,

Embellished in the window like a queen dressed for church.

All the "oohs" and "aahs" followed by those not picked on the hill,

Now over the jealousy of being left out in the chill.

They longed to be like her and hoped time would pass

Until they would get their chance to be dressed up at last.

But our tree couldn't handle the anxiety anymore.

He said, "This is no honor; it is only torture!"

He claimed she didn't look happy and that this was barbaric.

"Glorified taxidermy!" he screamed, then fell into hysterics.

"We are such fools!" he cried out loud.

"We've lived for this and made this custom proud!

The farmer has raised us with these backwards ideas.

But we'd trusted him to care for our souls and free us.

We were so naive to fall for this as we did.

We can't reverse the hands of time. But we can find a way to live.

There must be some way, if we all stick together;

We will figure this out and in turn live forever."

Nobody made a sound, there was no agreement.

They were all so brainwashed, they couldn't believe it.

Our tree was upset he couldn't get them to see what was real.

He had to make them understand it was fear they had to feel!

"Look through the window!" he yelled to the bunch.

"Our old friend looks thirsty and her pines could crunch!"

"She is dead, they have killed her, look at her chest!

Her heart no longer pounds; they have made her Christmas

DEATH!"

The others just looked at him as if in a daze.

They believed he'd lost his mind and become crazed.

Like a lightning bolt going off in a flash in his head,

"I know how to beat them from something the farmer said!

Bald trees are unwanted, it's fullness we attempt to achieve,

So come on, everyone, we must pull out our leaves!

I know you are scared of how much this will hurt,

But it will never hurt as much as having your roots long for dirt."

He began by the fistful ripping at his pine.

"They will never take us, don't worry, we will be fine."

The others just stood there and watched him with fright.

They couldn't believe they were witnessing this tonight.

It wasn't that they had any fear of the pain,

What the tree began to realize was they were all much too vain.

From the day of their planting it was meant to be,

That good looks and beauty were their only priority.

They were disgusted by our tree and very much appalled.

"How could he be so stupid? He looks as if he were mauled!

He has stripped himself of all honor, depriving himself.

If we follow his lead, we'll become a bookshelf."

So, they all just kept watching the tree with disgust.

It was not the farmer, but the tree they began to distrust.

In one last effort our tree tried to plead.

"Please listen to me! It is human greed!

We must escape this death-monger.

If we band together, we can all live longer.

We will all look the same and no one will try.

We will be ugly together. But it won't matter because we survived."

But it didn't matter to the others, it was much too late.

They didn't want to be ugly and would rather accept their fate.

It was no use, our tree had no other options to explore.

He wept silently and watched his tears fall to the floor.

In that moment, he knew that, no matter what,

He would never give up even if he gets cut.

He knew being left behind he would be lonely and numb.

And that he would face the frost by himself. Until summer would
come.

He loved the others, they were his family, his friends,

But what good was that if they are accepting the end?

Thanksgiving was coming so that would mean

The men from the tree lots would come, as routine.

Weeks went by and he stayed there naked in the frost.

Destroying fresh growth on himself, knowing the cost.

Then the men came from the tree lots, ready for business.
With horses, trucks and saws getting their picks for Christmas.

"There is still time," he said before the men reached them.
"Please believe me! Look at their weapons of mayhem!
Saws of metal and steel cannot feel pleasant.
If you think time has run out, don't worry, it hasn't."

But all of the others just went on ignoring.
They told him he was a fool and he would become flooring.
So the tree looked around and said with much affection,
"I love you all and good luck with your inspections."

Within minutes the men were on the hill staking their claim.
Pulling bunches away by horses in harnesses and reins.
Down the hill the trees went all gasping for air,
Being pulled like plows behind great white mares.

Our tree closed his eyes and tried not to see,
As his friends were hacked down so ruthlessly.
His ears rang with horror with every crunch of their boots
And his spine felt a shudder as the men left the roots.
They were leaving nothing behind, one by one down each row.
Nearer the front, our tree had an hour to go.

The men pulled the others from all around.
It was a massacre, but no blood stained the ground.

All of his friends, those whom he loved,

Why didn't they listen to the ideas he shoved?

And then it occurred to our little tree sapling,

"What if I haven't prevented anything from happening?"

He felt panic and wished he could run for the street.

He even scorned nature for not giving him feet.

But that was so difficult while around him was killing.

He was so broken it felt like his heart was spilling.

But he stood there until one man stood at his side

Inspecting our tree open-mouthed and wide-eyed.

"Did you see this ugly thing? Is it even a spruce?

Is it even worth the time to cut loose?"

Another man chimed in, "Yeah, it looks like hell.

It looks like a mollusk, minus its shell!"

The man laughed at our tree as he waited for the response.

Our tree felt suffocated like he wore a corset of the Renaissance.

"Oh please don't pick me, don't bother cutting me down."

He felt his mind leave his body before he heard a faraway sound.

Like a sound had been echoed lightyears through time.

Our friend heard the response as if from Heaven's clock keeping time.

"Be careful with that one and try not to touch it,

It looks diseased and won't bring us a profit."

With that the man stepped around and moved on to the next.

The executioner had passed him, but was set on taking the rest.

Several more were cut down and then the job was done.

The men had taken them all. All except one.

They were all dragged away and he was all alone,

With just stumps around him like remnants of bone.

What was he to do now, just wait for the spring?

Then more would be planted and go through the same thing.

He was cold and lonely, and the wind hit his face.

He hated himself for being stuck in this place.

But there was the deal he'd made not that long ago,

That if he could beat them he could face the snow.

Some time had passed, but he knew not how long,

When the farmer came to his hill humming a song.

But it was still too early, Christmas had yet to pass.

Snow still covered his roots, the dirt and the grass.

"What is the farmer doing? Why is he here?"

The little tree gagged while he choked on his fear.

As the light reflected off the metal of the farmer's saw,

The little tree realized he had escaped nothing at all.

"Christmas didn't happen yet, not for another week

A family must still need a tree. There was no mistake!"

The farmer would chop him down to his end.

Do you remember him saying that to the sapling's old friend?

But this seemed different, something was off.

The farmer said, "You made it," in a low muffled scoff.

"This will take a while, the ground is quite frozen.

Your path is a bit different than the usual one chosen."

He lacerated the ground with a shovel and his foot,

And began to dispose of earth just around the root.

Much time progressed as the farmer worked around him.

"They are paying extra for you. From the rough they've found a
diamond."

Our sapling was despondent and could only feel defeated.

All of his ideas, attacks and resources were depleted.

But what the farmer was doing was unusual to understand.

"Why is he digging and blistering up his hands?

And why? How? What would they want with me?

I am bald and unfit for Christmas aristocracy!"

The tree had many thoughts such as these in that moment,

And that he didn't want to be from royal Christmas descent.

But the time had come and there was no use in fighting.

He was loose from the ground and bid the hill his tidings.

He was pleasantly surprised that his lungs still had oxygen

And his heart was still beating, in that he was certain.

He was dragged down the hill by his sappy tree trunk,

Then delicately loaded into the farmer's rusty red truck.

It felt horrifying having his roots exposed to the frost.

It was violating and absurd and all his hope had been lost.

The farmer secured him in tightly with some rope and a knot.

Then he hopped in the truck and started for the tree lot.

They pulled out the driveway, out onto the road,

But the tree was still shocked that he was about to be sold.

Then all at once the blood rushed to his head.

He began hyperventilating at the thought of being dead.

He was very claustrophobic and began to reach panic.

He was beyond paranoid and was now in the realm of manic.

He struggled and fought and tried to free himself from the twine,

As the truck turned the corners up a steep mountain incline.

If he could just loosen the straps, he could squirm his way off the truck.

He would roll down the hill and land in a snow bank with luck.

"What good would that be?" he soon realized.

"Without the ground there is nothing to be photosynthesized.

I'll starve out there out in that remote wilderness.

No one will save me, I will accomplish no success."

Then all of the sudden the truck began to yield.

They were in town, just before the tree-selling field.

As they waited for the color of light to turn emerald,

Our little tree friend received a sight to behold.

He saw a mass of trees in the distance not far in advance.

He realized it was his friends and they looked to be in a trance.

They stood there motionless, their boughs creaking in the wind.

They all had closed eyes, looked breathless, tired and thin.

Some were from his farm, but with others he was not acquainted.

None were still breathing, their lives had been tainted.

It was a death field towards which he was embarking.

He would yet remain alone despite trees surrounding.

He longed for his hill, his friends and his family.

"I should have gone with the others," he said to himself gravely.

"Then I would have been with them, I'd not die alone.

What I wouldn't give now for the chance to atone.

I was happy where I was before I became neurotic.

I've hated these thoughts, wish I'd been blindly patriotic.

But I guess all of that is too late for me now.

I must resume my dignity and take my final bow."

Then in an instant he became fatigued, with a slower pace.

A warm glow covered his entire body and he at once felt peace.

Accepting his situation he'd given up his fight.

If he could conserve his energy, he might just live through the night.

He closed his eyes and remembered the sound of his mother's soft voice.

His breathing became deeper and his needles no longer felt moist.

He was content, now not concerned about anything but rest.

He drifted off, then gently awoke when he felt warmth across his chest.

"I must be in Heaven," he thought as he opened his eyes.

"It is so warm and lush here and there is light in the skies."

His mind was still drowsy, it was foggy and unclear.

"Am I still with the farmer? Is that him in the mirror?"

His mouth was dry as cotton and he was so completely exhausted.

He was trying to regain control, but fell asleep again and lost it.

He was awakened for the second time. But this time to a conversation.

Then the truck finally stopped, they must be at their location.

But the tree was confused. Nothing was familiar.

Where were all his friends? It was so peculiar.

Where was the tree lot? And where was the snow?

He was so tired though, it no longer mattered to know.

Then the back of the truck opened with a loud thud,

And a different man, not the farmer, pulled him out in the mud.

"What is going on here? The air is as fresh as spring."

There were enormous trees around him filled with birds that could sing.

He was set on a blue blanket and pulled across the lawn.

All around him was life, nature and a deer with her fawn.

Then the man pulling him stopped at the edge of a great field.

The tree was confused. "This isn't a tree lot. Why did he yield?"

As our tree was lifted into a crevice deep in the ground,

He began to freak out and look frantically around.

"But why would I be here, I'm so scrawny and crispy!

The farmer must want me healthy. So next year Christmas won't miss me."

This didn't stop the man from burying him in the cavity.

When his roots tasted the earth. They forced deep towards gravity.

"I don't know what's happening. How could this be?

I'm not dying at all. This man has saved me."

Looking around, all to see was dense wilderness,

Hundreds of the grandest trees of every different lineage.

These great organisms had roots intertwined in the earth.

Their trunks were one hundred times his size. He couldn't believe

their girth.

Their hearts beat as one somewhere under the ground.

That is what it's like for giant beasts as these. So he heard around.

Nothing was frightening, this did not seem wrong.

His panic was melting and his fear was soon gone.

The man packed the clay at the bottom of his trunk tight.

While doing so a megalith tree started talking to our tree at his

right.

"Welcome to our forest," said the Great Old Oak.

His voice rumbled and echoed off the mountains as he spoke.

"You have come just in time, there is much work to be mastered.
Our work is most important. We are priority in this pasture."
"Excuse me, sir, I don't quite follow your vocabulary.
What work am I capable of? I'm weak and arbitrary!"

"You, my little friend, are capable of great work, you see,
For hundreds of years you will help the world to breathe."

"But I should be dead. I don't know where we are.
I started at a Christmas tree lot and then loaded in a car."

The oak boomed a laugh and then became quite somber.
He told our sapling to look behind him over his shoulder.
Our tree had ended up underneath a large advertisement again.
But this one was quite different. It said people would come to visit
him.
Again the sapling had questions, he could not comprehend.
He couldn't wrap his mind around why anyone would visit him.

The ancient oak advised him he was missing his intention.
"Read it again," he insisted, "but this time pay attention."

Welcome
to the
Arboretum

"Congratulations, my boy, you have achieved freedom."

In bold black letters it said, "WELCOME TO THE ARBORETUM!"

"But Oak, the word arboretum, that's foreign to me."

"Oh well, my son, it simply means tree sanctuary."

"You mean I did it, I made it, I'm not going to die?

I'm free to grow and grow til my branches scrape the sky?"

"Yes, you deserve this, we've all heard of your strength.

The wind whispered to us that you refused to walk the plank."

For the last time in the story the tree began to cry,

"Besides, that's what the sign says, and why would it lie?"

The story goes that our sapling
lived on until the end of the earth,
All because he chose his own path
and recognized his self-worth.

Made in United States
Orlando, FL
30 September 2024